P9-DGR-133

ZOOM! ZOOM!

SOUNDS OF THINGS THAT GO IN THE CITY

COFFEE

WRITTEN BY
ROBERT BURLEIGH

ILLUSTRATED BY
TAD CARPENTER

A Paula Wiseman Book
Simon & Schuster Books for Young Readers · New York London Toronto Sydney New Delhi

SIMON & SCHUSTER BOOKS FOR YOUNG READERS · An imprint of Simon & Schuster Children's Publishing Division · 1230 Avenue of the Americas, New York, New York 10020 · Text copyright © 2014 by Robert Burleigh · Illustrations copyright © 2014 by Tad Carpenter · All rights reserved, including the right of reproduction in whole or in part in any form. · SIMON & SCHUSTER BOOKS FOR YOUNG READERS is a trademark of Simon & Schuster, Inc. · For information about special discounts for bulk purchases, please contact Simon & Schuster Special Sales at 1-866-506-1949 or business@simonandschuster.com. · The Simon & Schuster Speakers Bureau can bring authors to your live event. For more information or to book an event, contact the Simon & Schuster Speakers Bureau at 1-866-248-3049 or visit our website at www.simonspeakers.com. · Book design by Jessica Handelman · The text for this book is set in Helvetica Neue. · The illustrations for this book are rendered digitally. · Manufactured in China · 0514 SCP · 10 9 8 7 6 5 4 3 2 · Library of Congress Cataloging-in-Publication Data · Burleigh, Robert. · Zoom! Zoom! : Sounds of things that go in the city / Robert Burleigh ; illustrated by Tad Carpenter. · p. cm. · "A Paula Wiseman Book." · Summary: From morning's joggers until night's last train, a boy notices and enjoys the many sounds made by people and things in a big city. · ISBN 978-1-4424-8315-6 (hardcover : alk. paper) · ISBN 978-1-4424-8316-3 (eBook) · [1. Stories in rhyme. 2. Noise—Fiction. 3. Sound—Fiction. 4. City and town life—Fiction. 5. Vehicles—Fiction.] I. Carpenter, Tad, ill. II. Title. · PZ8.3.B9526Zoo 2014 · [E]—dc23 · 2012041015

For Jeff and Jackie—go for it!—R. B.

To Kansas City—the city I love to love—T. C.

The city is asleep.

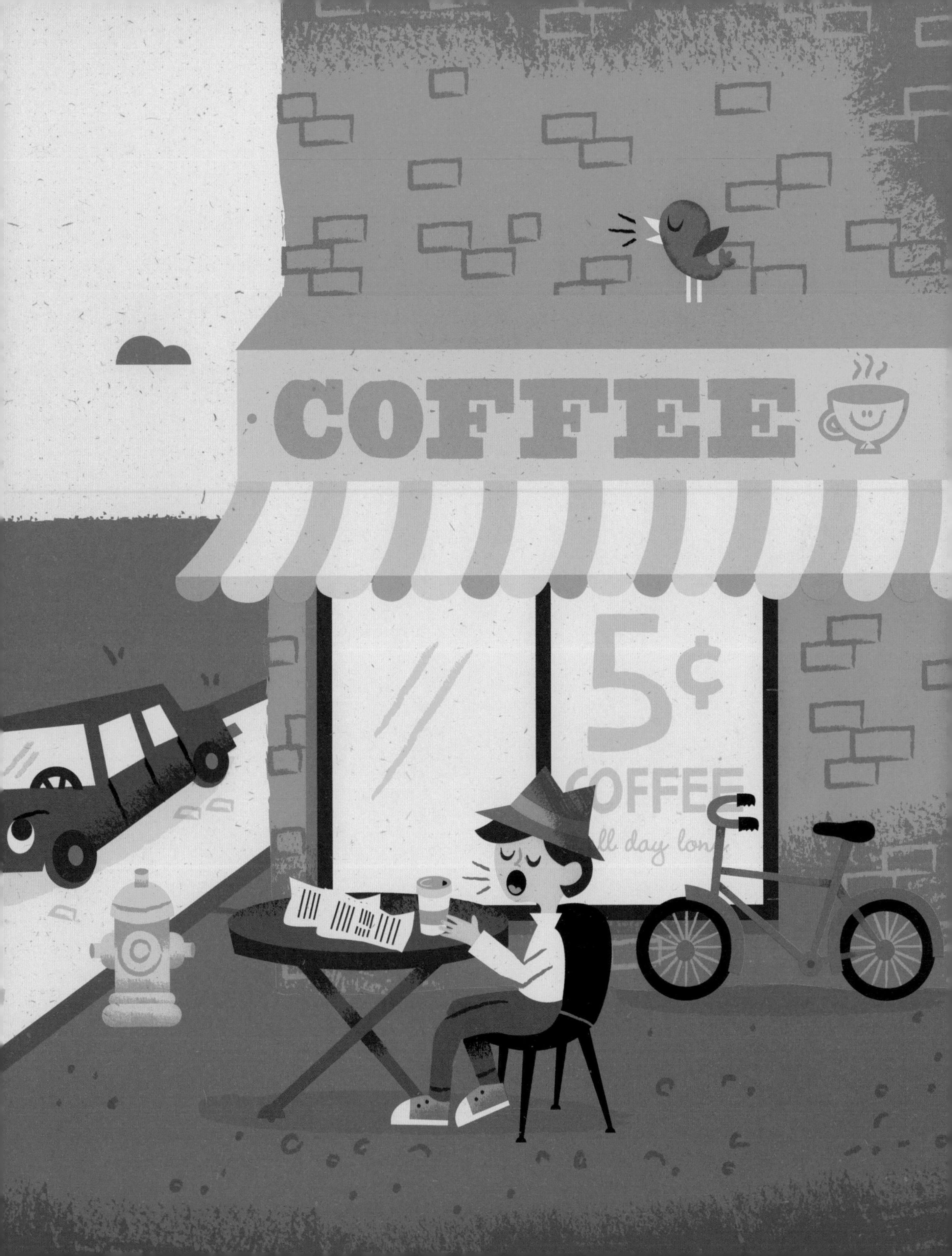
COFFEE
5¢
COFFEE

Shake up, City.
Let's get moving.
Hey, everyone.
Let's get grooving.

Night is over.
Sun's aglow.
Garbage trucks. Joggers.
Time to go.

Good morning, City!

HUSTLE BUSTLE!
RUSH-RUSH-RUN!

Cars in traffic
sway and swerve.
Over. Under.
Watch that curve.

Convertible, ambulance,
limousine.
Red light, orange light,
yellow, green.

Work time, City!

Vans, pickups,
cement trucks too.
Easy does it.
Coming through.

Juice it up.
We're in a hurry.
Get it finished.
Scurry, scurry.

Good job, City!

DART! DASH!
DART-DIVE-DASH!

Catch an el train.
Way up high.
Bricks and windows
flashing by.

Watch the wheels
whirl and spin.
Riders out
and riders in.

Lunch time, City!

yum!

RATTLE! RATTLE!
RATTLE-RATTLE-ROLL!

Look. Yikes.
A fire truck.
Wheeling. Reeling.
Whee. Good luck.

Firemen race
to save the day.
But we can't stop.
We're on our way.

Go, City!

Bus comes rocking.
Whoops. Jump.
Squeeze inside.
Sit down. Bump-bump.

Step on it, Driver.
Show some speed.
Rock it. Roll it.
Take the lead.

School's out, City!

SAVE GA

RUMBLE!
RUMBLE!
RATTLE-
RATTLE-ROLL!

SPIN! SPIN!

WHOOSH-

WHOOSH-

Hop the subway.
Way below.
Tunnels winding.
Go-go-go.

Rip and roar,
but we don't care.
Whatever works.
Just get us there.

Play time, City!

WHOOSH!

Downhill, uphill.
Skateboard flipping.
Whir and whiz. Spin.
Get zipping.

Motorcycle.
Rubber burning.
Lean left, lean right.
Twisting, turning.

Fun time, City!

Through the park
to the other side.
Bicycle whirring.
What a ride.

Ice cream truck music—
feel the beat.
Get me home.
It's time to eat.

Dinner time, City!

yum!

ICE CREAM!

RING! RING!
BUMP-BOUNCE-BOP!

Hail that taxi
zooming by.
Let's go, Cabbie.
Let it fly.

City hopping.
Razzamatazz.
Neon flashing.
Jive and jazz.

Party time, City!

Tired dancers
slowly walking.
Subway riders
softly talking.

Last train empties.
Day winds down.
All is quiet
in the town.

Sleepy time, City.

SHUFFLE. SHUFFLE.
WHISPER-WHISPER-

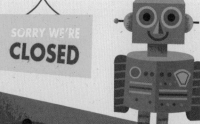

Good night.